C

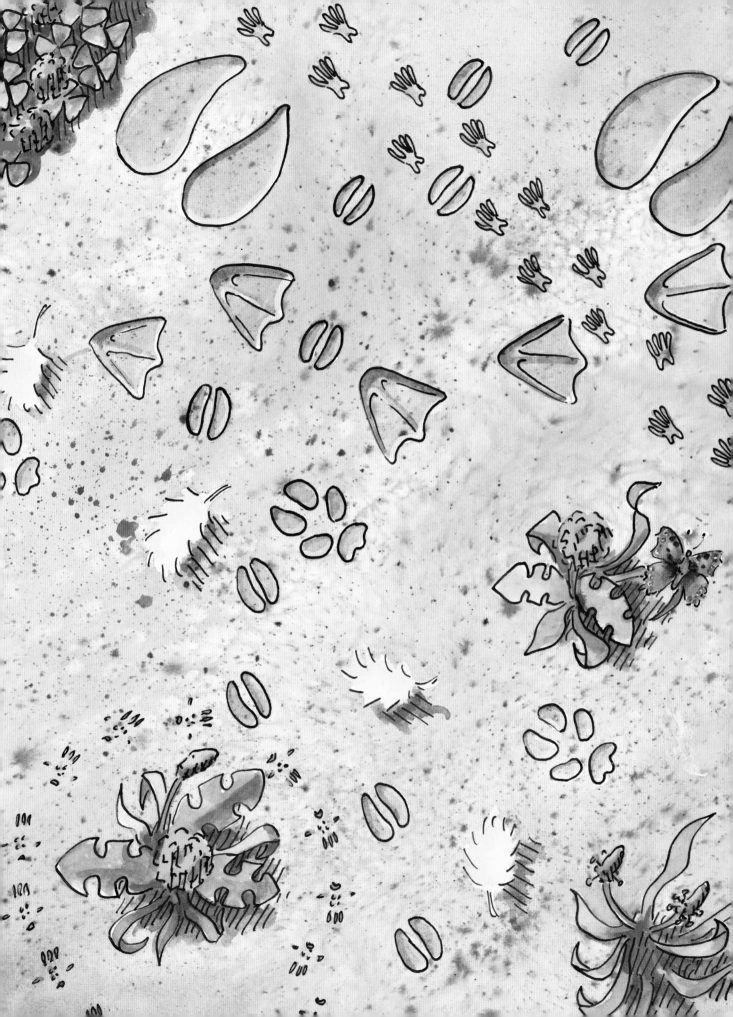

This book is for my dad, Roland Smith,
who told us all about Bella and Gertie.

Ladybird books are widely available, but in case of difficulty may be ordered by post or telephone from:

Ladybird Books – Cash Sales Department Littlegate Road Paignton Devon TQ3 3BE
Telephone 01803 554761

A catalogue record for this book is available from the British Library

Published by Ladybird Books Ltd Loughborough Leicestershire UK
Ladybird Books Ltd is a subsidiary of the Penguin Group of companies
©LADYBIRD BOOKS LTD MCMXCVI
The author/artist have asserted their moral rights
LADYBIRD and the device of a Ladybird are trademarks of Ladybird Books Ltd

BELLA & GERTIE

by Geraldine Taylor
illustrated by Guy Parker-Rees

Picture
Ladybird

The whole farmyard was in uproar.
The geese were hissing, the ducks' feathers
were standing on end and the donkey had
'hee-hawed' so many times he was hoarse!

Something dreadful had happened during
the night. The hen house was empty and
every single hen had vanished without
a trace.

All the animals were calling for Bella and
Gertie, the world-famous private detectives,
to find the culprit and solve the mystery.

"We'll go to the scene of the crime and look for clues," said Bella. "But we'll have to make sure that nobody sees us."

"I'll put on my dark glasses," said Gertie. "Then no one can see me."

"And I'll wear my detective hat," said Bella. "And no one will be able to see me either."

"I've found a clue," said Gertie. "Someone has opened the hen house door. We must find out who did it."

"I'll ask the questions," said Bella, "and you listen to the answers, Gertie."

"*I* didn't open the door," said the horse.

"*I* didn't open the door," said the bull.

"*We* didn't open the door," said the sheep.

"And it certainly wasn't *me*," said Foxy.
"I've hurt my paw—I can't go round
opening doors. Look how Mrs Foxy's
bandaged me up!"

"These muddy footprints are a clue," said Bella. "We'll have to ask you all to show us your feet."

"They're not *my* footprints," said the rabbit.

"They're not *my* footprints," said the horse.

"They're not *our* footprints," said the geese.

"Well, they certainly aren't *my* footprints," said Foxy. "Look, I have to wear my black boots. Mrs Foxy gets cross if I come indoors with muddy paws."

"Did any of you hear strange noises in the middle of the night?" asked Bella.

"We did!" cried the sheep. "We heard a horrible howl and we almost jumped out of our wool!"

"That's a clue!" said Gertie. "We must find out who howls in the middle of the night."

"*I* can't howl," said the goat.

"*I* can't howl," said the turkey.

"*I* can't howl," said the donkey.

"And *I* certainly can't howl," croaked Foxy. "I've got a dreadful sore throat. Mrs Foxy makes me wear this scarf to keep it warm."

Bella and Gertie examined the ground with their magnifying glasses. Suddenly, Gertie cried, "I've found a trail!"

Sure enough, there was a trail of feathers leading from the hen house through the gate and into the field.

"Follow those feathers!" cried Bella.

Bella carefully followed the trail…
all the way into the pond!

"Someone is trying to make us look
ridiculous," said Bella. "Well, it won't work.
We're world-famous private detectives.
We'll set a trap."

That evening, the farmyard was in uproar again because there was a notice on the hen house door. It said:

"How could the farmer get new hens when we don't know what's happened to the old ones?" cried the donkey.

"Why can't Bella and Gertie solve the mystery and get our friends back?" hissed the geese.

But Bella and Gertie said nothing.

That night, the cow detectives kept watch at either end of the hen house…

Suddenly, in the moonlight, a shadow crept up to the hen house and carefully lifted the latch. Gertie slammed the door shut and cried. "I've trapped the criminal – it's a shadow! I've never trusted shadows!"

But Bella peeped through the hole in the hen house roof and cried…

"It's FOXY! It's FOXY pretending to be a shadow. It's Foxy without his boots, and without his scarf and HE'S GOT A GREAT BIG SACK."

"There aren't any new hens, Foxy!" said Gertie. "We've caught you in our trap! What do you say about that?"

"You've got nasty, suspicious minds," said Foxy sulkily. "I've brought a sackful of *presents* for the new hens. Let me out, I'm going home to Mrs Foxy. *She* knows what a kind, generous fox I am…"

"You aren't going anywhere until you tell us where you've hidden the hens," said Bella. "If you DON'T tell us, we'll go and get the farmer and you know what *he'll* do."

Foxy snarled, "They're in the old barn. I was keeping them for my birthday—a hen for every year of my age. Mrs Foxy was going to make such a wonderful stew."

And with that he jumped out of the hen house and ran home, giving the loudest, foxiest howl that anyone had ever heard.

The animals cheered when Bella and Gertie brought the hens home. They all agreed how lucky they were that the most famous private detectives in the world lived in a cow shed on their farm.

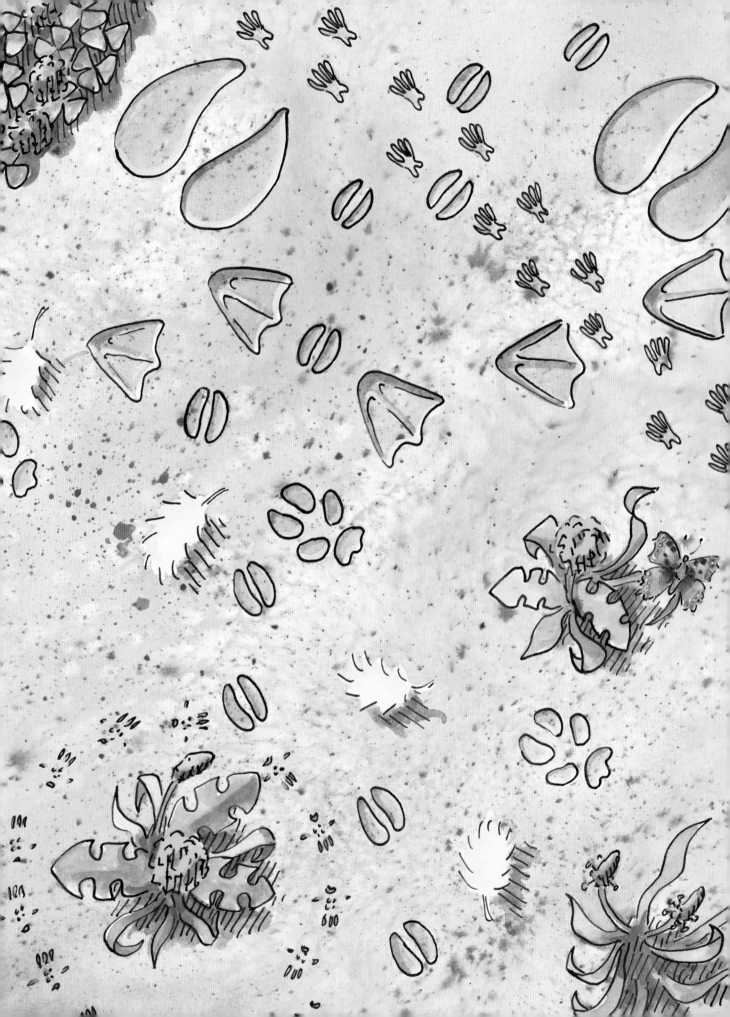

Picture Ladybird

Books for reading aloud with 2–6 year olds

The exciting *Picture Ladybird* series includes a wide range
of animal stories, funny rhymes, and real life adventures that are
perfect to read aloud and share at storytime or bedtime.

A whole library of beautiful books for you to collect

RHYMING STORIES

Easy to follow and great for joining in!

Jasper's Jungle Journey, Val Biro
Shoo Fly, Shoo! Brian Moses
Ten Tall Giraffes, Brian Moses
In Comes the Tide, Valerie King
Toot! Learns to Fly,
Geraldine Taylor & Jill Harker
Who Am I? Judith Nicholls
Fly Eagle, Fly! Jan Pollard

IMAGINATIVE TALES

Mysterious and magical, or just a little shivery

The Star that Fell, Karen Hayles
Wishing Moon, Lesley Harker
Don't Worry William, Christine Morton
This Way Little Badger, Phil McMylor
The Giant Walks, Judith Nicholls
Kelly and the Mermaid, Karen King

FUNNY STORIES

Make storytime good fun!

Benedict Goes to the Beach, Chris Demarest
Bella and Gertie, Geraldine Taylor
Edward Goes Exploring, David Pace
Telephone Ted, Joan Stimson
Top Shelf Ted, Joan Stimson
Helpful Henry, Shen Roddie
What's Wrong with Bertie? Tony Bradman
Bears Can't Fly, Val Biro
Finnigan's Flap, Joan Stimson

REAL LIFE ADVENTURE

Situations to explore and discover

Joe and the Farm Goose,
Geraldine Taylor & Jill Harker
Going to Playgroup,
Geraldine Taylor & Jill Harker
The Great Rabbit Race, Geraldine Taylor
Pushchair Polly, Tony Bradman